The Call of the Wild and Other Stories

The *Oxford Progressive English Readers* series provides a wide range of reading for learners of English.

Each book in the series has been written to follow the strict guidelines of a syllabus, wordlist and structure list. The texts are graded according to these guidelines; Grade 1 at a 1,400 word level, Grade 2 at a 2,100 word level, Grade 3 at a 3,100 word level, Grade 4 at a 3,700 word level and Grade 5 at a 5,000 word level.

The latest methods of text analysis, using specially designed software, ensure that readability is carefully controlled at every level. Any new words which are vital to the mood and style of the story are explained within the text, and reoccur throughout for maximum reinforcement. New language items are also clarified by attractive illustrations.

Each book has a short section containing carefully graded exercises and controlled activities, which test both global and specific understanding.

The Call of the Wild
and Other Stories

Jack London

Hong Kong
Oxford University Press
Oxford

Oxford University Press

Oxford   New York
Athens   Auckland   Bangkok   Bombay
Calcutta   Cape Town   Dar es Salaam   Delhi
Florence   Hong Kong   Istanbul   Karachi
Kuala Lumpur   Madras   Madrid   Melbourne
Mexico City   Nairobi   Paris   Singapore
Taipei   Tokyo   Toronto

and associated companies in
Berlin   Ibadan

Oxford is a trade mark of Oxford University Press

First published 1992
This impression (lowest digit)
5   7   9   10   8   6

Illustrated by K.H. Cheung, Reader
Syllabus designer: David Foulds
Text processing and analysis by Luxfield Consultants Ltd

ISBN 0 19 585269 9

Printed in Hong Kong
Published by Oxford University Press (China) Ltd
18/F Warwick House East, Taikoo Place, 979 King's Road,
Quarry Bay, Hong Kong

CONTENTS

1 THE CALL OF THE WILD: PART ONE   1

2 THE CALL OF THE WILD: PART TWO   9

3 ALL GOLD CANYON   20

4 TO BUILD A FIRE   27

5 THE ONE THOUSAND DOZEN EGGS   36

6 LOVE OF LIFE   44

   QUESTIONS AND ACTIVITIES   53

CONTENTS

1. THE GIST OF THE WORLD PART ONE
2. THE GIST OF THE WORLD PART TWO
3. ALL GOOD GIVERS
4. TO BUILD A FIRE
5. THE ONE THOUSAND DOZEN
6. LOVE OF LIFE

QUESTIONS AND ACTIVITIES

THE CALL OF THE WILD:
PART ONE

From California to the North

Buck was a very happy dog. For four years he lived at Judge Miller's house in warm southern California. Buck had a lazy, pleasant life. Then one day Manuel, the Judge's gardener, lost all his money, and Buck's life changed. 5

Manuel knew Buck was big and strong. He also knew some men who would pay a lot of money for a good dog. These men needed large, strong dogs to help them with their work in Canada, far to the north 10 of warm southern California. One sunny day Manuel stole Buck. He put a rope around Buck's neck and took him away from his happy home. Manuel sold Buck to two men named Perrault and François. They took Buck on a train going north. 15

Buck was very unhappy. He didn't understand what was happening to him. And he didn't like the rope around his neck. When he pulled, the rope hurt his throat. He was 20 very angry.

For two days and nights Buck travelled north on the train. At last the train stopped and the men pushed Buck out. Buck 25 stood and waited. The air was cold in this strange place.

The rope was still around his neck. The men were talking and laughing with other men at the railway station. Buck was sad and very angry. He pulled on the rope. Perrault and François told him to stop
5 pulling. But he pulled on the rope again and again. Then it happened.

Buck saw François holding a stick in his hand. Buck played with sticks at the Judge's house. He thought François was going to play a game with him.
10 But François held the stick above Buck's head and brought it down on him. Buck didn't know what had happened. He felt the pain of being hit with a stick for the first time in his life. He was angry and he tried to bite François. This was a mistake. François hit him
15 with the stick again and again. The pain hurt and Buck's mouth was bleeding. Buck learned he could not win against the man, the stick and the rope. He sat down, and the men laughed at him.

The men bought another dog named Curly. Then
20 they left the train station and went to the place where a boat waited for them. The men got on to the boat, followed by Buck and Curly. They were on their way north again.

Curly was a pleasant dog and Buck sat with him
25 in a corner. François brought another dog to sit with them. He was called Dave. Dave was not at all pleasant. He wanted to be left alone.

The days passed as the boat moved towards the North. Buck felt the air around him become colder
30 and colder as each day passed. Each day on the boat was the same. The dogs ate and slept. One day, Dave stole Buck's supper. Perrault saw what Dave did. He hit him with the stick. Buck hated Perrault but he thought he was right to hit Dave.

One day the boat slowed down and stopped. The men put the ropes on the dogs and led them off the boat. Buck stepped off the boat and felt something like mud on his feet. It was wet and cold. It was not really mud. It was a white colour. He felt some cold white bits hitting his face. He tried brushing them away but the bits disappeared before he could hit them. The men watched Buck and laughed at him. Buck didn't know that he was in the land of snow and ice. He was standing in snow for the first time in his life.

The land of snow and ice

Buck's easy life was over. François and Perrault were his new owners. He had to do what they told him. They often hit him with a rope or a stick. Soon Buck learned something else about life in the North.

On their first day in the land of snow and ice, Buck and Curly met some other dogs. François and Perrault were their owners, too. Curly tried to make friends with one of them. The dog was angry. It attacked Curly. Soon the other dogs attacked Curly. In a few minutes poor Curly lay on the ground covered with blood. He was dead.

Buck was frightened and sad. He didn't understand why the animals killed his friend. He was angry, but he knew he couldn't fight all the dogs at one time. And fighting was new to Buck.

François pulled Curly's body away. Then Perrault put some things around Buck's neck. Buck had seen something like them before. The horses at the Judge's house wore them when they worked. It was a harness, fastened on an animal's neck to make it pull things.

Buck was put in a line with the other dogs and together they pulled a large sledge. François and Perrault drove the sledge. They whipped the dogs to make them go faster and faster. This was new to
5 Buck. It was hard work. The sledge was heavy and the ground was cold on Buck's feet.

A dog called Spitz was the leader. When Buck went the wrong way he felt the whip on his back or the bite of the dog beside him. Buck was tired and angry but he wanted to live so he did as he was told.

They pulled the sledge all day. At last Perrault and François stopped the dogs and
15 made a camp for the night. Buck was hungry and tired. His feet hurt from running on the hard, icy ground. He ate his supper of raw meat quickly. It was not cooked, but it tasted good. After supper the other dogs went away. Buck was so cold
20 and there was no place for him to sleep. There was

only snow. He looked around the camp. The other
dogs were gone. Then he heard noises coming from
under the snow. He dug the snow away and there
was Spitz, sleeping. That night Buck learned how
animals slept in the North. He dug a hole and sat   5
down in it. Soon he was covered with snow. Soon he
felt warm, and he slept all night.

And so the days went by. The dogs pulled the
sledge forty miles each day across the snow and
ice. Buck learned to pull the sledge. He learned   10
to fight for his food. He learned to get angry and
show his teeth to the other dogs. Slowly, he was
becoming a wild animal. As time went by, Buck
couldn't remember much about the Judge or warm,
sunny, southern California. He wanted to live. And   15
to live in the North he knew he must become the
strongest dog of all.

Buck and Spitz

The men and the nine dogs had to travel five hundred
miles. Buck did his job. Each day he pulled the   20
sledge. He became stronger and stronger. Spitz, the
leader, didn't like Buck. Spitz knew Buck wanted to
be the leader of the dogs.

At the end of one long day, the dogs sat down to
go to sleep. Buck and Spitz were angry with each   25
other. Both dogs knew they would soon fight to the
death.

Then the dogs heard some noises. They moved
from their holes in the snow to see what was
happening. They saw their food being eaten by a   30
group of strange dogs. François, Perrault, and the
nine dogs ran to the food tent.

The strange dogs were very hungry. There were about thirty of them. They were eating the food as quickly as they could. Buck had never seen dogs like these. They were so thin that you could see their
5 bones under their skin.

Buck and the others attacked the strangers. But the 'thirty thieves' were so hungry they didn't run away. A fight started. François and Perrault hit the strange dogs with sticks. But the dogs got much of the food.
10 Then they ran from the camp. Buck, Spitz and the other seven lay in the snow, tired and bleeding.

Buck learned that hungry dogs will do anything to get food.

15   Perrault and François let the dogs rest for one day after the fight. When the dogs felt better they started on their five hundred mile journey again. Day after day they pulled the sledge.
20 Sometimes Spitz tried stealing Buck's food. Buck would attack but François always stopped the two dogs from fighting. The other seven dogs knew that there would soon be a big fight. It was very simple.

Buck wanted to be the leader of the dogs. One day it happened.

Buck was walking around the edge of the camp. Spitz attacked him. He bit Buck's throat, then his face. Buck was angry, very angry. It was time for the fight. 5

Both animals knew it was a fight to the death. Buck ran at Spitz. Spitz pulled away then jumped on Buck's back and bit his neck. Buck knocked him on to the ground. He put his teeth into Spitz's neck and killed him. 10

The other seven dogs came to Buck and licked him. Buck stood and looked at the other dogs. He was their new leader. He was the wildest and strongest dog of all.

A change of job 15

The next morning Perrault and François looked for Spitz. They saw Buck's bleeding neck and they knew Buck had killed Spitz to become the leader. But François put another dog at the front. The dog, Soleks, was frightened of Buck and moved away. 20
Buck had won the fight with Spitz. He wanted to be at the front. At last, François and Perrault gave Buck his way.

With Buck in the front, the dogs went twice as far each day. He loved his job. Each day he made the 25
others move faster and faster. Buck led the dogs to the town of Skagway, and his job with François and Perrault was finished. The men said goodbye to the dogs and sold them.

Buck and the other dogs were sold to mail carriers. 30
The mail carriers' job was to move the mail across the most dangerous paths in the North. The mail was

heavy. Buck didn't like this work. Each day was the same. Buck led the others as they pulled the heavy mail sledge across the snow and ice. The dogs ate fish. They missed the meat François and Perrault had fed them.

Sometimes at night Buck would sit by the fire and look at the flames. He would think about the lazy days at the Judge's house and feel sad. But now he was a leader of dogs. That made him happy.

The days went by and the work was hard. All the dogs grew thin. Dave was the first to become ill. He was a good dog. He always worked hard, but he was tired. His feet and legs hurt and he cried from the pain. Buck helped Dave by pulling harder. One day Dave fell down. Then, the next day, he fell again.

The men talked about Dave. They knew he was ill. One morning he couldn't move at all. The men led the other dogs away from the camp. Buck and the others watched one of the men go back to where Dave was lying in the snow. They heard the shot from the gun. Buck and the others knew what had happened to Dave. The man had shot him and he was dead.

Buck was sad about Dave's death. He thought of how important it was to be the strongest dog. He wanted to live. He knew he must always be the strongest dog of all.

THE CALL OF THE WILD: PART TWO

Charles, Mercedes and Hal

Thirty days after Dave was shot, the mail job was over. But the dogs were very tired. They had lost weight and needed a rest. The mail men sold Buck and the other dogs to three people who wanted to go on holiday. The mail men said goodbye to Buck. 5

Charles, his wife, Mercedes, and Mercedes' brother, Hal, were the new owners. These three had never been on holiday in the North before. They knew nothing about travelling with dogs across the ice and 10 snow. They should have given the dogs a week's rest. But they were very silly travellers.

They put too many things on the sledge. Mercedes had too many clothes. Charles didn't bring enough dog food. The tired dogs tried to pull the sledge. It 15 wouldn't move. Charles hit them with a whip. The dogs tried again. The sledge moved, then it fell over. It was too heavy. They took off some of the things and the sledge was lighter. At last they left on their holiday. 20

Buck was very tired, but he did his job. The first night at camp Charles and Hal tried to put up their tent. Buck watched them. The tent fell. They tried again. Buck knew these people were new to the North. Mercedes gave the dogs too much food. Buck 25 watched and he knew this was going to be a hard journey.

In a few days the dog food was almost all eaten. Mercedes was cold. She didn't like this holiday. Charles and Hal knew they had made a mistake in taking this holiday but they

5 couldn't turn back. By this time the closest town was very far away.

10 It was the beginning of spring in the North. It got warmer and the snow and ice started to melt. Buck felt this under his feet. He knew they should not travel on the

15 frozen river. He knew it was dangerous. He knew they could fall through the ice and die. But Charles made the dogs travel on the frozen river.

John Thornton

The long days went by. The travellers were unhappy.

20 The dogs were hungry and unhappy too. One day they came to a camp. It was the camp of a man named John Thornton. He had two dogs called Skeet and Nig.

John Thornton welcomed the tired travellers. He saw the dogs. He watched Charles, Mercedes and Hal. He knew they were silly travellers. The dogs looked almost dead. He gave Charles, Mercedes and Hal some hot coffee. John Thornton was a good man. He was sad when he looked at the dogs.

Charles said goodbye to John Thornton. He stood and told the dogs to move. Buck was so tired. He didn't move. He wanted to die. Charles hit Buck with the whip. This made John Thornton very angry. He jumped and took the whip from Charles.

'What are you doing, Thornton?' said the angry Charles.

'If you hit that dog again, I'll kill you,' said John Thornton. He held his knife in his right hand.

'It's my dog,' said Charles. Mercedes was crying and Hal was frightened.

'The dog stays with me,' said Thornton. He looked at poor Buck.

Charles knew that Thornton was a man of the North. He could fight, and win.

'All right, you can have the dog, Thornton,' said Charles. 'He's no use to us. He's almost dead.' He and Mercedes and Hal wanted to leave. The other dogs moved slowly. They went to the sledge. Buck was still as he lay on the ground.

'You're silly to travel on the river,' said Thornton. 'The ice is melting. It's dangerous.'

But Charles was a silly man. He and the others left and went down to the river. Thornton knew they would go through the ice. He turned and looked at poor Buck.

John Thornton looked for broken bones on Buck's thin body. He rubbed Buck's back and legs. He

gave him some meat and sat with him. John
Thornton's dogs, Skeet and Nig, licked Buck's feet.
Then the man and the three dogs heard a noise.

5   It was the sound of ice breaking, and men and
animals screaming. Thornton and the dogs knew that
Charles, Mercedes and Hal and the dogs were all
dead. They had gone through the ice.

    Buck didn't understand what was happening to
him. This man was good and kind. The other dogs
10 were licking him. They were not angry. He opened
his eyes and looked at the kind face of John Thornton.
Why was he taking care of Buck?

Buck is happy again

John Thornton looked after Buck because he loved
15 animals. He loved all animals. But he loved the dogs
of the North best. He knew they had a hard job and
he knew some men were unkind to the dogs. As he
looked at poor Buck he thought about the man who
had hit him. This made him very angry.

20   For two weeks John Thornton took care of Buck
day and night. He fed him and kept him clean. And
he loved him. Skeet and Nig
slept close to Buck to keep
him warm. Slowly, Buck
25 became strong
again.

It had been a long time since anyone had loved Buck. At first he watched John Thornton. At any minute he thought the whip or the stick would come down on him. It didn't. Thornton gave Buck the first real love in his life. The Judge had been kind to Buck, *5* but he hadn't loved him as Thornton loved him.

Soon Buck could stand and run. Skeet and Nig played games with Buck. John Thornton threw sticks for the dogs to catch. The three dogs and Thornton went for long walks around the camp. The dogs ate *10* good raw meat. In a few short weeks, Buck loved John Thornton. He had never loved a man before. He licked Thornton's face, he sat with him, he wouldn't leave his side. Buck was so happy. He loved Skeet and Nig, too. *15*

Buck's love grew and grew. He would sit by the fire each night and watch John Thornton. He would move closer and closer to this man he loved. He put his head on Thornton's leg, and he was happy.

Buck saves John Thornton's life *20*

The weeks of early spring went by. As soon as Buck could travel, John Thornton and the dogs left their winter camp. Thornton was going to meet his friends. He had a small sledge and the three dogs pulled it.

They travelled by the side of the river for one *25* week. The spring had arrived and the river melted. They stopped by the river one day and waited for Thornton's friends.

In a few days John Thornton's friends arrived by boat. Their names were Pete and Hans. They brought *30* the boat to the side of the river and picked up John and the dogs. Buck was not kind to Pete and Hans until he saw they were John Thornton's friends. They travelled on the river to the town of Dawson. Here they bought food, then started on their journey.

This was a happy journey. The three men were
5 friends. The dogs were friends. And Buck loved John Thornton. Thornton put a large bag on Buck's back. He would carry anything for John Thornton.

Buck was a wild dog. His love for Thornton didn't stop Buck being wild. He ran off to the woods at
10 times, but he always returned to Thornton.

The group travelled through the summer. It was a pleasant journey until the accident.

They were travelling along the side of the river. John Thornton fell into the water. The river was
15 strong. It pulled him away. Buck jumped into the water. He swam and swam. He pulled as hard as he could. He pulled John Thornton from the river. Buck saved John Thornton's life.

John Thornton looked at Buck and tears came to
20 his eyes. He thought, 'This is the best dog, and friend, I've ever had.'

The journey continued. Buck watched John Thornton all the time. He wanted John to be safe. He ran by his side. Pete
25 and Hans thought Buck was a good dog, too. They knew he was the strongest dog in the North and they knew he loved John Thornton.

Buck wins some money

They travelled all summer and autumn. They arrived at Dawson again. The men needed money to buy a sledge for the winter and Buck won the money. This is how it happened.   5

John Thornton and his friends told some other men that Buck could pull a sledge with one thousand pounds on it. The men laughed. They knew that very strong dogs could pull seven hundred pounds but not one thousand pounds. The men told John Thornton   10 they would give him sixteen hundred dollars if Buck could pull one thousand pounds on a sledge. The men were very silly.

John Thornton talked to Buck. Then he put a harness around Buck's strong neck. Buck pulled. The   15 sledge didn't move. John spoke to Buck again. Buck pulled and pulled. He knew John Thornton wanted him to move this sledge. The sledge moved very slowly at first, then faster and faster.

The men were very surprised. They had watched   20 many dogs in the North but they had never seen one as strong as Buck. They gave John Thornton the money. John Thornton looked at Buck. Buck had won sixteen hundred dollars in five minutes.

John, Pete and Hans bought a new sledge, food   25 and warm clothes with the money. They were ready for the next journey.

Looking for gold

John bought other dogs because the sledge was heavy. The men knew it would be a long journey.   30 They were going north. Far to the north. Many men had tried to make this journey. They had all died. Men wanted gold. Many of these men had lost their lives looking for gold. And the most gold was found in the far north.

5   John Thornton and his friends wanted gold. They had heard a story about a lost gold mine in the far north. They knew many men died looking for that gold mine. But they wanted to try. They harnessed the dogs. Buck led with Skeet and Nig behind. The
10 new dogs followed the leaders. They left Dawson.

They travelled north. Day after day they pulled the sledge. Not many men went as far north as these men. Buck was happy to pull a sledge for John Thornton.

15   Sometimes they would stop for one week. Buck watched the men go to a stream of water and look for something. He didn't know what gold was. The men looked for the gold. If there was no gold, they started north again. After travelling for a few weeks
20 they would stop again.

Buck sat by the fire at night. Sometimes he heard new and different sounds. The sounds came from the woods. They were the sounds of an animal. Buck had never heard these sounds before. He did not know
25 what kind of animal made them. When they came, John Thornton held his gun in his arms.

Wolf leader

When the dogs stopped pulling the sledge for a week, Buck and the others had little to do. The other
30 dogs would play games, but Buck went into the forest. He loved the woods. One day he saw an animal. It looked like a dog but Buck knew it was

not a dog. Buck was a killer. He ran after the animal. But the wild animal turned and rubbed his nose to Buck's. It was a wild wolf. The wolf was smaller than Buck. Buck could have killed it. He didn't. He made friends with the wild wolf. They ran together through   5
the woods. Then Buck returned to the camp, he returned to John Thornton.

Buck wanted to be with John Thornton. He also wanted to run and hunt with the wild wolf. He felt the wolf was his brother. In the day he would run   10
with the wolf. At night he returned to the camp, to John Thornton. Once he stayed away all night with the wolf. But he returned to John in the morning.

The men found gold. Large pieces of gold. They made camp and stayed for weeks. Buck went into   15
the woods and hunted with the wolf. He met other wolves. They were his friends. One day he ran with the wolves. He ran and ran. They hunted other animals.

Three days went by. Buck remembered John   20
Thornton and he ran for many miles back towards the camp. He smelled something in the air. And he was frightened.

One mile from the camp, Buck found Nig. He was dead. Nig had a bullet hole in his side. Then he found the other dogs. They were all dead, too. He was frightened.

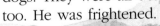

One hundred yards
from the camp he saw them.
There was John Thornton, dead.
Pete and Hans were dead. Everyone was dead.
5 Indians were dancing around John Thornton's fire.

Buck was angry. The most angry he had ever been.
The Indians had killed John Thornton. Buck's heart
was broken. He wanted to kill them.

He jumped on the first Indian and bit his neck
10 open. The Indian died. He killed another Indian, then
another. The Indians who were still alive ran into the
woods; they had never seen an animal so wild.

Buck sat by John Thornton and howled. This is the
way dogs cry. He howled and howled. The hours
15 went by. Then the wolves arrived. Buck looked at
them, angrily. They yelled to Buck. He called back.
Then he stood and went to the wolves. He yelled
louder than all the others. He was stronger than all

the others. Buck became
the leader of the wild wolves of
the North. He was a wolf, now.

   Buck led the wolves in the hunt. He
ran many miles each day. Sometimes he went back to   5
the camp and howled for his friend, John Thornton.
He would think back to the games and love he had
had with John Thornton.

   But then he stood up and went to his new job,
again. Buck was the leader of all the wolves in the   10
North. He was the strongest one of all.

3

ALL GOLD CANYON

Summer in the North

The canyon was a beautiful place. It was between two high mountains. The trees were green there. The flowers were many different colours - white, yellow, blue and red. There were pools of clean water in the deep canyon.

It was summer in the North. The snow melted and the flowers grew quickly. It was sunny and warm. Butterflies and other insects came to the canyon. It was a happy place.

The animals loved the canyon. They drank the clean water and smelled the beautiful flowers. Birds sang there all through the day.

Then the animals heard a man. They heard him singing as he came to their canyon. The animals knew men killed them, so they ran away. The man came down the side of the mountain into the canyon.

He was alone on this sunny day. His feet made a noise on the rocks. He wore heavy shoes. His hair was yellow. He was a happy man and he sang songs. Two horses followed the man into the canyon. They carried his food, clothes and his tools. The man was a gold miner.

There were many men like this in the North. They went from one place to another place looking for gold. They knew gold would make them rich. Some men would kill for gold.

The man came to this canyon to look for gold. He
wanted to be rich.

He looked around the canyon. He saw it was a
beautiful place. He was a happy man and he sang as
he took his tools from a large bag on the back   5
of the horse.

The tools were a shovel and a pan.
The man went to work with his tools. As
he worked he talked to himself, often. He looked   10
around the canyon and said, 'It smells good here.
Now, I'll see if I can find some gold.'

Gold dust

He took his shovel and pan and went to one of the
pools of water. He put his pan in the water. Then,   15
he pushed the pan against the bottom of the pool.
A gold miner's pan has small holes in the sides. Water
and mud came in through the holes. He took the
pan out of the water and looked at the black and
brown mud at the bottom. He pushed the mud   20
around with his fingers. Nothing.

He moved to another place along the edge of the
pool and did the same thing, again. This time there

was another colour in with the mud. It was yellow.
The man laughed. 'I knew this was a good place,' he
said.

5   He washed the pan and pushed the mud away from
the yellow part. 'This looks like gold to me,' he said.

It was gold dust. The man knew he had found
the right place. He stood and looked around the
canyon again. He looked at the rocks on the side of
10   the canyon walls. 'There's gold in those big rocks,
and I'm going to find it,' he said. He was very happy.

It was late in the afternoon. The man knew he
should stop and eat, but he was too happy to stop
looking for his gold. He knew that if there was gold
15   dust in the water then there was a lot of gold
somewhere in the rocks.

The man went to another pool of water and found
more gold dust. Then another, and another. Soon it
was dark and he stopped his work.

20   The man built a fire and cooked his supper. Then
he fed the two horses and went to sleep. Before
he went to sleep he said, 'Good night, canyon.
Tomorrow I'll find the gold you're hiding in the
rocks.' He slept all night.

The next day

25   In the morning the man woke and cooked his
breakfast. Then he took his tools and went to work
again. He put the pan in another pool. There was a
lot of gold dust in this pool. The man knew he was
near to the big pieces of gold. He sang as he picked
30   up his shovel and hit it against some rocks.

He hit the rocks again and again. Pieces of rock
fell on the ground. He picked up one of the pieces

and hit it with the end of the shovel. It broke and he saw a thin line of gold in the rock. He laughed and laughed. Then he sang.

The man worked through the morning. By twelve o'clock he had some pieces of gold, good gold. 5

At twelve o'clock he stopped to rest. He fished and caught two big fish. He built a fire and cooked them. He ate his lunch, then went to find more gold.

He worked through the afternoon. He sang and talked to himself as he worked. Soon it was dark. 10

The man stood up and looked around. 'It's night! I didn't see it get dark,' said the man. He laughed. Then he cooked his supper, ate it and fed the horses. He slept all night.

He worked the next day. And the following day. 15 Then, he found the best gold yet.

'Great!' he yelled. He had found big pieces of gold. He got a bag and filled it with the gold. Many large pieces. The man knew he was rich. Very rich.

'I'm holding forty thousand dollars in gold in my 20 hands,' he said. He sang and sang.

The next day he was at one edge of the canyon looking for more gold. In front of him was one of the biggest pieces of gold he had ever seen. But something was wrong. 25

He was frightened. He didn't look up. He looked at the wonderful gold. But he knew something was very wrong.

Another miner?

He heard a sound. It was a small sound. He told 30 himself it was a bird. But he knew that was not true. It was the sound of a man.

He did not look up. He was too frightened. Then it happened.

He felt the pain as soon as he heard the noise. It was the noise from a gun. The bullet came from
5 behind him and hit him in the back. The man fell to the ground.

The stranger at the top of the canyon looked down. He looked at the man for a long time. He put away his gun for a minute. Then he took it out again.

The stranger sat there for a long time. He watched the body below. It didn't move. He could see what he wanted. The gold!

The man thought the gold miner was dead. He climbed down the side of the canyon. He moved slowly towards the miner's body. The body lay over the biggest pieces of gold. So the killer went to move the miner's body.   5

A thief!

Suddenly, the miner pushed the stranger away.

'I'm not dead! You thief! You shot me in the back!' yelled the miner. He jumped on the stranger and tried to get the gun from his hand.   10

Both men held the gun. A bullet shot into the air.

'You thief!' yelled the miner.

The men hit each other again and again. Another bullet shot into the air.

The miner was very angry. He didn't feel the bullet   15
in his back. He wanted to kill this man who had shot him.

At last the miner had the gun. He shot the stranger. He shot him again and again until there were no more bullets. The body fell on the gold. Then the   20
miner felt very tired. He lay on the ground.

He felt his back. The bullet had gone through his back and out the other side. He held his shirt against the hole in his back. He knew he would live. It was not a dangerous bullet hole.   25

He looked at the dead body on the ground.

'You shot me in the back, you thief,' he said to the body.

Then the miner stood up. He took his shovel and pushed the body into a hole. Then he covered the   30
hole with earth. He was very tired. He picked up his gold and put it in the bag.

The miner built a fire and cooked his lunch. He ate, then he fed the horses. He put the gold on the horses' backs. Then the miner turned and looked at the canyon again.

5 'Goodbye,' he said to the canyon. 'Goodbye,' he said to the dead man. He climbed the side of the canyon with his horses and his gold.

The canyon was quiet. Then the animals came back. The birds sang. And beautiful green grass grew
10 over the place where the dead man lay under the ground.

The beautiful canyon was a quiet and happy place again.

TO BUILD A FIRE

A very cold day

The day was cold and grey when the man left the path to Yukon City. He turned off to the east, a path not often used. It was nine o'clock and there was no sun. There were no clouds. The sky was grey. He didn't care. He hadn't seen the sun for many days.

He looked back. The long river Yukon was covered with three feet of ice. On top of the ice were three more feet of snow. The river ran many miles north and south. To the south it led to Chilkoot Pass. To the north it led a thousand miles to the Bering Sea.

The man did not think much about the river on that grey day. He was new to this land and this was his first winter. It was fifty degrees below zero. The man knew it was very cold. But he did not know what the cold could do to a man's body.

He knew it must be about fifty degrees below zero. 'That's all right,' he thought. 'The temperature is not important.' He was going to the camp at Henderson Creek. The other men were already there, waiting for him. He would be at the camp by six p.m., a bit after dark. There would be a fire and a hot supper. As for lunch, he carried it inside his shirt. It was the only way to keep his lunch from freezing.

He passed the trees and started walking along the path. It was not a clear path because a fresh foot of snow had fallen. He was glad he did not have his sledge. The only thing he carried was his lunch. He

was surprised by the cold. 'It really is very cold,'
he thought. He had a large beard, but this did not
cover his cold red cheeks or his nose.

A big grey dog walked beside the man. The dog
was not happy on this day. The animal knew it was
5   far too cold to be travelling. The dog didn't know
anything about temperature or degrees. It just knew it
was very, very cold. The dog knew fire and it wanted
to be near to a fire now.

The man and the dog walked for four or five miles
10 and then came to some water. This was Henderson
Creek. The man looked at his watch. It was ten
o'clock. This was good. He was moving along
quickly; by half-past twelve he would be at the Forks.
He kept walking and planned to eat his lunch when
15 he got to the Forks.

There wasn't anyone to talk to, but the man didn't
care. It would have been hard to speak with the ice
on his beard. 'It is so cold,' he thought.

Sometimes he rubbed his cheeks and nose with his
20 mittens. The rubbing didn't help very
much. The minute he took his
hand away from his face
his nose and cheeks felt as
cold as ice.

The man was very careful as he walked along. Henderson Creek was frozen, but he knew there was icy water hiding under the ice. This cold water would make his feet wet. Wet feet were dangerous in this temperature. He would have to stop, build a fire and dry his socks and shoes. He did not want to do that so he was very careful.

For the next two hours he made the dog walk in front of him. The dog was not very pleased about this, but did as it was told. Suddenly, the dog broke through the ice and got its feet wet. It tried licking the water from between its toes but the water changed into ice very quickly. The man helped by pulling the ice from the dog's toes. Then they moved along.

Lunch time

At half-past twelve the man and dog arrived at the Forks. He was happy with the speed he had made. If he kept going at that speed he would arrive at the camp by six o'clock. He undid his coat and took out his lunch. He felt the cold, icy air on his fingers when he pulled off his mitten.

He took a sandwich and put it to his mouth. He tried to eat. But his beard was frozen. He couldn't move his mouth. He had forgotten to build a fire and melt the ice from his beard. The man smiled. He knew he had been silly.

He put on his mitten and stood up. He was a little
bit frightened and he jumped up and down until he
could feel his feet. 'It is very cold,' he thought. When
he had been walking his blood had been moving
5 through his body. But the minute he stopped his
blood moved more slowly. His feet and hands were
the first parts of his body to feel it. He knew he must
keep moving. He rubbed his nose. It was freezing.

But he was safe. He worked carefully with some
10 small pieces of wood, laying them on top of each
other. He started a fire and fed it with larger and
larger sticks. Soon it was burning brightly. It melted
the ice in his beard and he could eat his sandwiches.
The dog warmed itself by the fire, and all was well.
15 After a while he called to the dog and they started on
their way.

An accident

They had been walking for half an hour. He had not
seen the black, icy water. It happened suddenly. The
20 snow and ice under his feet broke open. He fell
through into the cold water. 'That was stupid of me,'
he thought. He had been careless. Now, he was wet
to his knees.

He was angry at his mistake. The man knew he
25 would have to build another fire and dry his shoes
and socks. And he knew, now, he would be late
arriving at the camp.

The dog watched the man start making another
fire. The man lit a few small sticks. The fire caught.
30 Soon he would put larger sticks on it. He would take
off his wet shoes and socks and dry them over the
fire. Then everything would be fine.

Soon the flames of the fire danced in the cold air. He started to take his shoes off. They were covered with ice and he could not undo them. He took out his knife. Then it happened.

He knew what he had done as soon as it happened. He should not have built the fire under the tree. He should have built it in the open. The tree was heavy with snow. Each time he pulled a branch off to feed the fire, he moved the tree. Then something moved high up in the tree. It was snow, falling off one of the branches. The snow from that branch fell on to another branch, then another. Suddenly, all the snow from the tree fell down through the branches and on to the fire. The fire went out.

The man was surprised. He knew he could die because of this. He looked at the place where the fire had been. 'I must build another one,' he thought. He knew he must not make any mistakes this time. 'My feet must be frozen,' he said to himself. 'But there's no time to think about them now.'

Another fire

The man was busy. He tried not to think about his feet. He was building the new fire in the open. The dog watched him. It knew that men made fires, but
5 this man took a long time with his fires. The dog waited.

The man tried picking up some small sticks but his freezing hands could not feel them. He could not feel his feet. The dog sat in the snow and watched the
10 man. The man stood and jumped up and down again. He waved his arms about trying to make the blood run through his body. He wished very much that he was the dog with its thick, warm, coat.

The jumping helped to move the blood and he
15 felt his fingers. He picked up some sticks. Then he took off a mitten and took out the matches. His fingers quickly lost their feeling. He tried taking one match from the others but all the matches fell in the snow. His fingers couldn't pick them up. He put on
20 his mittens and hit his hands against his legs. Some feeling came to his fingers and he got hold of the matches.

The man held the matches between his hands. His beard was frozen and his
25 mouth hurt as he made it open. He put the matches in his mouth and moved one match away from the others. He sat down on the snow. He held the match in his mouth and rubbed it
30 against his leg. He rubbed the match twenty times before it lit. The match burned his mouth and he dropped it in the snow.

The man wished he wasn't alone. Suddenly he took off both mittens. He picked up all the matches together and rubbed them along his leg. Seventy matches caught fire at once. He looked at the flame in his hands. His skin was burning. He could smell it. In a few seconds he felt the burning and the pain.

He dropped the matches on the fire he had built. The flame fell on the sticks and the fire started. The man was very careful. He put small pieces of wood on the fire. One by one, he pushed them on. Then one stick that was larger than the others fell on the tiny flames. He watched it fall and move the burning sticks away from each other. Each stick stopped burning. The fire went out.

The man looked at the dog. He thought he would kill the dog and warm his hands inside the dog's body. Then he could build another fire. He spoke to the dog. The dog knew something was different in the man's voice and it moved away.

Death!

The man sat up in the snow. He then stood up and called to the dog in a pleasant voice. The dog came towards him and he held it in his arms. His arms ached with cold and he knew he could not kill the dog. He let go. The dog ran, then stopped forty feet away.

The man was afraid of death. He began running along the creek. The dog followed. The more the man ran the better he felt. He thought if he could keep running he could get to the camp. He also thought that if he stopped, he would die because of the cold.

His thought of running all the way to the camp was silly. In his heart he knew he could not run all that way. He fell down. When he tried to get up he fell again. 'I must rest,' he thought. As he sat in the snow he suddenly felt warm. But when he touched his cheeks and nose he could not feel them. And he could not feel his feet, or his legs. He knew his body was freezing. He was afraid. He pulled himself up and ran again. The dog followed.

The man looked at the dog and was angry. He yelled at the dog because he knew the dog wasn't freezing to death. After running another hundred feet he fell into the snow. He knew he was going to die. He was stupid to run about like this.

Suddenly he felt sleepy. 'I will fall asleep, and die,' he thought. His eyes closed and he began to dream. He was out of his body looking down at himself. He saw the men finding 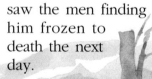 him frozen to death the next day.

The dog watched as the man fell asleep. It looked at the man and waited for him to get up and build another fire. But the man was very quiet, and didn't move. The animal moved closer. It smelled death and moved away.

5

The dog then turned and ran up the path. It went towards the camp where it knew there were other men with fires and warm food.

THE ONE THOUSAND DOZEN EGGS

A clever plan

David Rasmunsen lived in California. He wanted to make a lot of money. He heard stories about the North. He knew a man could make a lot of money if
5 he was clever. He knew there were many men working up North and they wanted the things of home. One of the things they wanted was – eggs.

David Rasmunsen could buy eggs for fifteen cents a dozen (twelve). The eggs would sell for five dollars
10 a dozen in the town of Dawson, far to the North. All he had to do was move the eggs up North. One thousand dozen eggs would cost him one hundred and fifty dollars. He could get five thousand dollars for them. The journey would cost him about eight
15 hundred and fifty dollars, or a bit more. He would bring home four thousand dollars. David Rasmunsen was very happy with his clever plan.

'I can do it, Alma!' he said to his wife. They sat at the table looking at maps. 'It will cost fifty dollars to
20 go to Dyea. At Dyea I will pay some Indians to carry the eggs to Lake Linderman. That will cost about two hundred dollars. At Lake Linderman I will buy a boat for three hundred dollars. I'll take some people across the lake. That will pay for the boat. The boat will
25 arrive in Dawson. I'll sell the eggs and get my money!'

Alma was not very happy with her husband's plan. But she knew he was going to go to the North with his eggs.

'The journey will take two months, Alma. I'll make four thousand dollars in two months! I only make one hundred dollars a month, now. It will be wonderful for us,' said David Rasmunsen.

David Rasmunsen got one thousand dollars from the bank. Then he bought one thousand dozen eggs. He said goodbye to Alma. He and his eggs got on a boat in San Francisco.

The sea journey was not pleasant. The water was rough. The boat travelled north. At the end of the summer David arrived at Dyea.

Lake Linderman

He spoke to the Indians about carrying his eggs to Lake Linderman, twenty miles away. The Indians said it would cost fifty cents a pound. David Rasmunsen thought it would cost twelve cents a pound. He was angry. But there he was in Dyea with one thousand dozen eggs. He had to move the eggs to Lake Linderman, so he paid fifty cents a pound to the clever Indians.

The Indians carried the eggs to Lake Linderman. A camp where men built boats was near the lake. David saw the men working quickly. They worked quickly because it was now autumn. Soon the winter would arrive. The lakes and rivers are covered with ice in the winter. The men wanted to sell the boats they had built before the winter came. The air already felt cold.

David did not have much money left, but he found people who paid him to take them across the lake. With this money he bought his boat.

Rasmunsen, his eggs, and the other people left Dyea in the boat. It was very cold. The wind blew

water on to the boat. There was ice in the water because it was so very cold. The waves were rough. He looked at his eggs. He thought the rough journey would break them. But they were all right. It was very
5   cold, but Rasmunsen was happy. His eggs were safe.

The lake was twenty-five miles wide. When they were twenty miles across, they saw large pieces of ice in the water. The last five miles were very rough. The ice, the wind and the water hit the little boat,
10   again and again. At last they came to the other side of the lake. David Rasmunsen was very tired. Then, the bad news came.

A terrible journey

The river to Dawson was frozen. This was very bad
15   news for David. He had planned to cross the lake, then take the boat on the river to Dawson. Now, the river was frozen. He could not take the eggs by boat to Dawson.

He would have to go on foot. He went to a bank in
20   the town. He begged the bank manager for money. He told him about his eggs and the good price he would get for them in Dawson. The bank manager let Rasmunsen have fifteen hundred dollars. If he did not pay it back he would have to give his house in
25   San Francisco to the bank.

Two weeks later he left for Dawson. He had three sledges, each pulled by five dogs. He drove one sledge. Two Indians drove the others. He looked at the eggs again. They were not broken. He smiled to
30   himself. His luck had not been good. But his eggs were safe.

The journey was a terrible one. Rasmunsen knew little about the North. The Indians were angry. They tried to tell the man how to travel in the North. He would not listen. He wanted to arrive at Dawson as quickly as he could. He pushed the dogs too hard. 5 They needed to rest because they were pulling a large number of eggs. But Rasmunsen made them go on.

One day his foot went through the ice. It got wet. The Indians knew this was dangerous. They tried to 10 make him stop, build a fire and dry his shoes and socks. He would not stop. A few hours later he couldn't feel his foot. It was frozen. He looked at it. Then he put a blanket around it and walked on. 15

Dawson, at last!

The Indians thought he was a very strange man. He worked harder than any other man they had seen. The Indians, who were men of the North, were very
5 tired. They wanted to stop and rest.

A few days later, the dogs began to die. Rasmunsen made them work too hard. He put the eggs from one sledge onto another. Now, he had three sledges, but only a few dogs.

10 One day one of the Indians fell into the icy river. He went under, and did not come up again. He was dead. That night the other Indian ran away. Rasmunsen tied the sledges together and went on.

The journey did terrible things to his body. His toes
15 had frozen. They were black and dying. The ice froze his face. His cheeks were black. His nose was black, too. But he wouldn't stop to rest and look after himself. He wanted to get to Dawson, to sell his eggs.

One day he met some men who were coming from
20 Dawson. They told him that Dawson was short of food. Then they saw his eggs. They said his eggs could be sold for one dollar each in Dawson.

'Twelve thousand dollars,' he said to himself, over and over again. He was sick and tired but happy. He
25 was going to make a lot of money on his eggs.

As he came closer to Dawson, more dogs died. He pulled the sledges the last miles with the few dogs he had alive. At last he arrived in Dawson.

'What a wonderful day'!

30 'What do you have in those sledges?' asked one of the gold miners in the town.

'Eggs,' said Rasmunsen. His face hurt. He could not speak easily.

'Eggs!' yelled the man. 'How wonderful. It's been a long time since I've seen eggs up here in the North!' Then the man went to tell the people in the town the good news. The men of Dawson wanted eggs very much.

Soon a crowd stood around Rasmunsen and his eggs.

'How much for the eggs?' asked one hungry man.

'One dollar and a half,' answered Rasmunsen.

'I'll buy one dozen,' said the man.

'They are one dollar and a half for each egg,' said Rasmunsen.

'That is a good buy,' said another man. 'I'll take a dozen, too.'

David Rasmunsen was so happy. It was the happiest day of his life. The town wanted his eggs. And they would pay one and a half dollars for each egg. 'What a wonderful day,' he thought.

The people crowded around him, buying the eggs. He sold a few dozen, then he felt sick. His head hurt. His whole body hurt.

'This poor man needs to rest,' said one of the men in the crowd.

'I know an empty house where you can rest,' said a man to Rasmunsen. 'Then we'll buy your eggs, after
5 you rest from your long journey.' The other people agreed.

So they moved David Rasmunsen and his eggs to a house on the edge of town. He took the eggs inside with him.

10 He was so very tired. He lay down for a while. He thought of his luck. And the money he would get for the eggs. He thought, 'The terrible journey is over.' He thought of all the things he would buy for Alma when he arrived home. He was very happy.

15 ## A broken heart

One hour later there was a knock on his door. The man who bought the first dozen eggs came into the house. He was angry.

'Your eggs are BAD!' said the man.

20 'What did you say?' asked Rasmunsen. His face looked frightened.

'I said, your eggs are bad. Bad, bad, bad!' yelled the man.

'My eggs. Bad,' said Rasmunsen. He felt sad and
25 afraid.

The man held the eggs under Rasmunsen's nose. They smelled terrible. The man was right. The eggs were bad.

'I want my money back,' said the man.

30 Rasmunsen gave him the money. 'Please go away. Get out,' yelled Rasmunsen. The man took the money and went away.

Rasmunsen was quiet for a long time. He looked at the boxes of eggs around him. Then he took his knife and went over to the boxes of eggs.

He cut open the first box. He took an egg and cut it open. It was black and green. It was bad. Then he took another box and cut open another egg. It was black and green, too. Then he took another, then another. And so on. Until he had cut open all the boxes of eggs.

The man was right. The eggs were bad. Very bad.

David Rasmunsen sat on the floor of the house. He cried as a baby would cry. All his money was gone. The bank would take his house. Alma would be so sad. His eggs were bad.

The terrible journey across the snow and ice had made him ill. His body was so tired. His heart was broken.

Rasmunsen stood up. He took a long piece of rope. He threw it over a large piece of wood up near the ceiling. He stood on a chair and tied the rope around his neck. He thought of Alma. Then he pushed the chair away. In a few minutes he was dead.

One of the men found him hours later. He went to the other men in the town. He told them that the Egg Man had taken his life. He said he thought Rasmunsen was a very silly man to kill himself just because of some bad eggs.

6

LOVE OF LIFE

A bad friend

The two men walked slowly down the hill. They were very tired and weak. They carried their things inside blankets tied on to their backs. Each man carried a gun.

'Soon we will be at the place where the food and the boat are,' said one tired man. The other man followed behind him. He didn't answer.

The two men came to a small river. They had to walk across it. The man who spoke went across first. The other man followed.

Suddenly, the other man fell into the water. He tried to stand up but his leg hurt. When he stood, he felt a pain in his leg. He couldn't move it.

'Bill, I've hurt my leg. I can't walk. Help me!' said
the man.

But Bill didn't stop to help his friend. He did not
turn around. He walked on through the water to the
other side of the river.   5

'Bill! Bill!' called the man standing in the river.
'Help me, Bill.'

Bill never looked behind him. He went on walking.
Soon he disappeared over the hill.

The man standing in the river was angry. His friend,   10
Bill, wasn't helping him. Bill was gone. The man felt
the pain in his leg. He knew he must get across
the river. He moved his leg. It hurt, but he walked
across the river. When he got to the other side he
fell down. He was very tired and his leg ached. He   15
stood and pulled himself to the top of the hill.

'Bill, Bill,' he yelled. But Bill was gone. And the
man was alone. He sat on the top of the hill and
looked around.

He was not lost. He knew the path. The path led   20
to the boat and food, waiting for him and Bill. 'Bill
will wait for me at the boat. He will be there when I
get to the boat,' he thought.

The way home

He looked at his gun. He didn't have any bullets. He   25
looked at his blanket. There was no more food inside
the blanket. Only a knife, a tin bucket and his gold.
He thought about the wonderful gold. He was rich.
He and Bill had found a lot of gold. Now, all he had
to do was go home. The boat would take them down   30
the river to town, then home.

He had not eaten for two days. He was very hungry. He ate some fruit which he pulled off a small tree. It didn't taste good.

He stood up and walked along. His leg hurt and
5 his stomach ached. He walked and walked. At nine o'clock he hit his toe on a rock. He fell down, very tired. He took his matches from the blanket and counted them.

Sixty-seven matches. He was careful with the
10 matches. He counted them again. Sixty-seven.

The man built a fire and dried his socks and shoes. His socks had holes in them and his feet were bleeding. He looked at his foot. It hurt. He tore a piece off one of his two blankets and put it around
15 his foot. Then he boiled some water and drank it. The hot water warmed his body. He lay down and went to sleep.

Nothing to eat

The man woke up at six o'clock. His
20 body hurt and his stomach ached. He was very, very hungry. He put his things in his blankets and carried them on his back.

25 He walked and walked. He wanted food. He heard some birds singing. He picked up stones and threw them at the birds.
30 He tried to kill a bird for food but the birds flew away from the man.

As he walked he saw wolves and bears and other animals. He was so hungry he tried to chase one of the wolves to catch it. The wolf ran away from the man.

He tried eating some leaves, but he was still hungry. In the afternoon he came to a pool of water. He saw some fish in the water.

They were very little fish, but they were food. The man tried to catch the fish with his tin bucket but the fish swam away.

He sat by the pool of water and cried. He cried because Bill had left him alone, because he was hungry and because his body hurt. He cried and cried.

Then he built another fire and boiled more water. He drank the hot water. He lay down under his blankets and went to sleep.

He felt very cold when he woke up the next morning. The man didn't watch where he walked. He just went anywhere. He ate some leaves that day. He lay down and fell asleep. The next morning was grey again. Cold and grey.

Food

In the afternoon the sun came out. The man looked around him. He knew he was lost. He turned and went another way. He found another pool of water. There were two small fish in the pool. This time he caught the fish with his tin bucket. He ate the fish. He walked until night. Then he slept again.

The days went by. Sometimes the man looked at his gold. The gold was very important to him. He and Bill had left warm California and come to the icy

North to find the gold. Sometimes the man wanted to lie down and die but when he thought about the gold he stood up and walked on and on.

One day he found a nest of baby birds. They were very small. He took four, and ate them.

Some days were very cloudy. It was difficult to see where he was walking, but he kept walking.

Each day he thought about food. At night he dreamed about food. He was not very strong. The blanket felt heavier and heavier. One day he threw away some of the gold. It was too heavy to carry.

Sometimes he dreamed he had one bullet in his gun. He would kill a wolf and eat it, if he had the bullet. But he had no bullet. Sometimes he dreamed he saw a horse in front of him. He got on the horse and rode away. But there was no horse. It was only a dream.

He saw a bear. A real bear. He ran after the bear. He thought he could kill the bear and eat it. The bear ran away from the man.

Sometimes he saw two or three wolves following him. He knew they were waiting for him to fall down. When he fell they would eat him. He didn't want to fall.

One afternoon he came upon the body of an animal the wolves had killed. There were only bones left. He looked at the bones. He took two of the bones and hit them against some rocks. Then he ate the bits of bone. The bones were hard. Some of his teeth 5 broke. But he ate the bones.

A ship

One day he came to the top of a hill. He looked down on a river. He saw something. At first he thought he 10 was dreaming, again. He rubbed his eyes and looked down again. He saw a ship. He saw the ocean. The ship was real. The man was very happy. But he was still a long way from the ship. And he was so very tired. Then he heard the wolf. It was five feet away 15 from him.

He watched the wolf. The wolf was old and sick. But it was hungry and it wanted to eat the man. The man knew the wolf wasn't strong. A strong wolf would have killed him by this time. The wolf was very 20 tired, but it watched the man.

The man looked at the ship again. He had to get to that ship or he would die. And he had to keep the old wolf from killing him.

The man pulled himself along for a while. He came 25 to some bones. He saw a blanket beside the bones. He saw the gold. The bones were his friend, Bill. The man felt sick and he pulled himself away.

The wolf followed the man.

The man stopped and sat for a few minutes. He 30 looked at his feet. They were bleeding. His blanket was gone. His gun and knife were gone. And the wolf followed the man.

The man moved slowly. One step, then another. He made his tired body move towards the ship. It was a long way from him. Once he sat and fell asleep. The wolf came very close to the man. But the man woke up and the wolf ran away.

He came to another pool of water. He caught one small fish and ate it. He felt stronger. He walked slowly towards the ship. And the wolf followed.

The strange animal

The days went by. Sometimes the man pulled himself along the ground. He looked at the ship, then at the wolf. He was two miles from the ship. He pulled himself along for one mile.

The man was very tired. He was almost dead. The wolf knew the man was tired. It waited for him to fall asleep. But the man wanted to live. He loved his life. So, he closed his eyes. He was not really asleep. He waited for the wolf.

The wolf walked to the man. It smelled the man's body. It licked the man's face. Then, it put its teeth to the man's throat.

Suddenly, the man put his hands around the wolf's throat. He was very tired but he knew he must fight the wolf. The wolf and the man lay on the ground. The wolf was old and tired but he bit the man's hands. 5

Then the man bit the wolf's neck. He bit as hard as he could. The man killed the old wolf. 10

After he had killed the wolf, he felt sick in his stomach. But he had to get to the ship.

The man left the wolf and pulled himself to the beach. The sand hurt his feet and hands. He pulled himself along the last mile to the ship. 15

The men on the ship saw an animal pulling itself along the sand. They watched the animal. Some of the men tried to guess what kind of animal it was.

Then one man yelled, 'It's not an animal, it's a MAN!' 20

The men went and got the man. He could not speak. He was almost dead when they took him to the ship.

He slept for days on the ship. One day he woke up and told the men what had happened to him. The men fed him.

At first, the man looked at the food. Then he ate 5 the wonderful food. The next day he ate again.

Soon, the man became fat. Then he became fatter and fatter. He could not stop eating. He ate and ate the wonderful food. 'Food is the most wonderful thing in the world,' he thought.

QUESTIONS AND ACTIVITIES

CHAPTER 1 (A)

Put the sentences in the right order to say what this part of the chapter is about.

1 They took Buck and Curly on a boat which went towards the North.

2 Perrault and François took Buck on a train going north.

3 When they got off the boat, Buck saw snow for the first time.

4 Buck travelled on the train for two days and nights.

5 Buck lived in southern California, at Judge Miller's house.

6 Then Perrault and François bought another dog called Curly.

7 One day the Judge's gardener stole him and sold him to two men.

CHAPTER 1 (B)

The letters in these words are all mixed up. What should they be? (The first one is 'hundred').

On the five (1) **denurdh** mile journey, Spitz was the (2) **ardele** of the dogs. Spitz didn't like Buck because Buck (3) **twenad** to be the leader.

Spitz (4) **daktatec** Buck when he was walking (5) **unorda** the edge of the camp. Spitz bit Buck's (6) **hottar** and face, and then he (7) **pudjem** onto his back. Buck knocked Spitz on to the (8) **odrung**. He put his (9) **hetet** into Spitz's neck and killed him.

The other dogs came to Buck and (10) **kidcel** him (11) **asecube** he was their new leader. Buck was the (12) **twisdel** and strongest dog of all.

CHAPTER 2

The underlined sentences are all in the wrong paragraph. Which paragraph should they go in? Write them out in the right place.

1   Buck heard some strange new sounds coming from the woods. <u>It looked like a dog, but Buck knew it was a wolf.</u> Buck did not know what kind of animal it was.

2   When Buck went into the forest he saw the animal. <u>He met other wolves and they were his friends.</u> Buck made friends with the wolf and they ran together through the woods.

3   Buck wanted to run and hunt with the wild wolf. <u>They were the sounds of an animal.</u> One day he ran with the wolves and they hunted other animals together.

CHAPTER 3 (A)

Use each of these words once to say what this part of the story is about: **noise, back, wrong, bird, canyon, pain, pieces, sound, gun, gold, bullet, ground, man, true.**

The next day he was at one edge of the (1) ____ looking for more (2) ____ . In front of him was one of the biggest (3) ____ of gold he had ever seen. But he was frightened. He knew something was (4) ____.

He heard a (5) ____. He told himself it was a (6) ____. But he knew that was not (7) ____. It was the sound of a (8) ____.

Then it happened. He felt the (9) ____ as soon as he heard the (10) ____. It was the noise from a (11) ____. The (12) ____ came from behind him and hit him in the (13) ____. The man fell to the (14) ____.

CHAPTER 3 (B)

Which are the true sentences about the man who came to the canyon?

1   (a) He had no shoes.   (b) He wore heavy shoes.

2 (a) He had brown hair. (b) He had yellow hair.
3 (a) He was a happy man. (c) He was a sad man.
4 (a) He had two horses. (b) He had one horse.
5 (a) He didn't find any gold. (b) He found some gold.
6 (a) He ate fish for lunch. (b) He ate fish for breakfast.
7 (a) He was shot in the arm. (b) He was shot in the back.
8 (a) He killed the stranger. (b) He helped the stranger.

CHAPTER 4 (A)

Put the ending of each sentence with its right beginning.

1 The man was going to ...   (a) he arrived at the Forks.
2 The other men ...   (b) and took out his lunch.
3 At the camp there would be ...   (c) his lunch inside his shirt.
4 He carried ...   (d) the ice from his beard.
5 At half-past twelve ...   (e) a fire and a hot supper.
6 He undid his coat ...   (f) because his beard was frozen.
7 He could not eat his sandwich ...   (g) were waiting for him there.
8 He had to build a fire to melt ...   (h) the camp at Henderson Creek.

CHAPTER 4 (B)

Choose the right words to say what this part of the chapter is about.

Suddenly the snow and ice under his feet (1) **froze over/broke open**. He knew he would have to build another fire to dry his (2) **shoes and socks/hat and coat**. Soon the flames of the fire danced in the (3) **cold air/white snow**. Then snow fell down from the tree and (4) **made the fire burn/put the fire out**.

He tried to pick up some sticks, but his hands could not (5) **feel/touch** them. He tried taking a match, but his fingers couldn't (6) **put it down/pick it up**. He held a match in his mouth and tried to (7) **light/eat** it. When it lit the match burned his mouth, and he (8) **broke/dropped** it.

The man took off both mittens and picked up all the (9) **branches/matches**. They all caught fire at once, and burned his (10) **skin/beard**. He dropped the burning matches on the fire and it (11) **went out/started**. Then a large stick fell on the flames, and the fire (12) **started/went out**.

CHAPTER 5

Put the words in the last part of these sentences in the right order so that they say what the story is about.

1 David Rasmussen went from ...   [boat] [Dyea] [by] [California] [to].

2 He paid some Indians to help him carry ...   [Lake] [the] [to] [Linderman] [eggs].

3 At Lake Linderman he bought a ...   [Lake] [boat] [to] [the] [cross].

4 When he got to the other side he found ...   [the] [was] [that] [frozen] [river].

5 He bought three sledges and some dogs ...   [him] [to] [take] [Dawson] [to].

6 On the journey one Indian died and ...   [one] [ran] [other] [the] [away].

7 Many of the dogs died, and so ...   [himself] [sledges] [he] [the] [pulled].

8 When he reached Dawson he discovered ...   [bad] [the] [were] [eggs] [that].

CHAPTER 6

Copy the table and write the answers in their correct places. The words going down in the centre will say what this story is about. Use these words: **leg, bones, shoot, leaves, fish, bucket, river, birds, eaten, bullets, friend, wolves, hungry.**

The man had fallen into the (1) ____ and hurt his (2) ____. He shouted to his (3) ____, Bill, to help him, but Bill went on walking. The man had a gun, but he had no (4) ____. He could not (5) ____ anything for food. He was very (6) ____. He had not (7) ____ for two days.

He picked up stones and threw them at the (8) _____ to kill them for food, but they flew away from him. Then he tried to catch some little (9) _____ with his tin (10) _____. The next day he just ate some (11) _____. Then, one afternoon he found the (12) _____ of an animal that the (13) _____ had killed. He broke them and ate the bits.

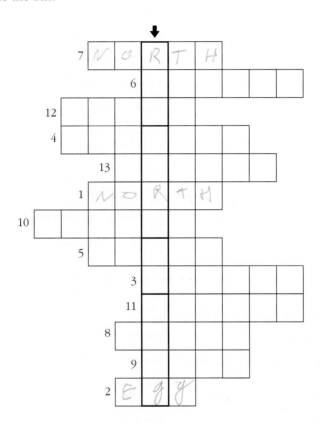

7 N O R T H
6
12
4
13
1 N O R T H
10
5
3
11
8
9
2 E g g

Oxford
Progressive
English Readers

GRADE 1

Alice's Adventures in Wonderland
Lewis Carroll

The Call of the Wild and Other Stories
Jack London

Emma
Jane Austen

The Golden Goose and Other Stories
Retold by David Foulds

Jane Eyre
Charlotte Brontë

Just So Stories
Rudyard Kipling

Little Women
Louisa M. Alcott

The Lost Umbrella of Kim Chu
Eleanor Estes

The Secret Garden
Frances Hodgson Burnett

Tales From the Arabian Nights
Edited by David Foulds

Treasure Island
Robert Louis Stevenson

The Wizard of Oz
L. Frank Baum

GRADE 2

The Adventures of Sherlock Holmes
Sir Arthur Conan Doyle

A Christmas Carol
Charles Dickens

The Dagger and Wings and Other Father Brown Stories
G.K. Chesterton

The Flying Heads and Other Strange Stories
Edited by David Foulds

The Golden Touch and Other Stories
Edited by David Foulds

Gulliver's Travels — A Voyage to Lilliput
Jonathan Swift

The Jungle Book
Rudyard Kipling

Life Without Katy and Other Stories
O. Henry

Lord Jim
Joseph Conrad

A Midsummer Night's Dream and Other Stories from Shakespeare's Plays
Edited by David Foulds

Oliver Twist
Charles Dickens

The Mill on the Floss
George Eliot

Nicholas Nickleby
Charles Dickens

The Prince and the Pauper
Mark Twain

The Stone Junk and Other Stories
D.H. Howe

Stories from Greek Tragedies
Retold by Kieran McGovern

Stories from Shakespeare's Comedies
Retold by Katherine Mattock

Tales of King Arthur
Retold by David Foulds

The Talking Tree and Other Stories
David McRobbie

Through the Looking Glass
Lewis Carroll

GRADE 3

The Adventures of Huckleberry Finn
Mark Twain

The Adventures of Tom Sawyer
Mark Twain

Around the World in Eighty Days
Jules Verne

The Canterville Ghost and Other Stories
Oscar Wilde

David Copperfield
Charles Dickens

Fog and Other Stories
Bill Lowe

Further Adventures of Sherlock Holmes
Sir Arthur Conan Doyle

Great Expectations
Charles Dickens

Gulliver's Travels — Further Voyages
Jonathan Swift